# Dear Parent:

Congratulations! Your child is taking the first steps on an exciting journey. The destination? Independent reading!

**STEP INTO READING®** will help your child get there. The program offers books at five levels that accompany children from their first attempts at reading to reading success. Each step includes fun stories, fiction and nonfiction, and colorful art. There are also Step into Reading Sticker Books, Step into Reading Math Readers, Step into Reading Write-In Readers, Step into Reading Phonics Readers, and Step into Reading Phonics First Steps! Boxed Sets—a complete literacy program with something to interest every child.

## Learning to Read, Step by Step!

**Ready to Read**  **Preschool–Kindergarten**
• big type and easy words • rhyme and rhythm • picture clues
For children who know the alphabet and are eager to begin reading.

**Reading with Help**  **Preschool–Grade 1**
• basic vocabulary • short sentences • simple stories
For children who recognize familiar words and sound out new words with help.

**Reading on Your Own**  **Grades 1–3**
• engaging characters • easy-to-follow plots • popular topics
For children who are ready to read on their own.

**Reading Paragraphs**  **Grades 2–3**
• challenging vocabulary • short paragraphs • exciting stories
For newly independent readers who read simple sentences with confidence.

**Ready for Chapters**  **Grades 2–4**
• chapters • longer paragraphs • full-color art
For children who want to take the plunge into chapter books but still like colorful pictures.

**STEP INTO READING®** is designed to give every child a successful reading experience. The grade levels are only guides. Children can progress through the steps at their own speed, developing confidence in their reading, no matter what their grade.

Remember, a lifetime love of reading starts with a single step!

www.stepintoreading.com

Educators and librarians, for a variety of teaching tools, visit us at www.randomhouse.com/teachers

*Library of Congress Cataloging-in-Publication Data*
Orr, Salile. One pink shoe / by Salile Orr ; illustrated by S.I. International.  p.  cm. — (Step into reading. A step 1 book)
SUMMARY: Barbie and friends count to ten and talk about their day.
ISBN 0-307-26106-9 (trade) — ISBN 0-375-99992-2 (lib. bdg.)
[1. Dolls—Fiction.  2. Counting.  3. Stories in rhyme.]  I. S.I. International (Firm).  II. Title.
III. Series: Step into reading. Step 1 book.   PZ8.3.O765  On  2003 [E]—dc21   2002013446.

Printed in the United States of America   23  22  21  20  19  18  17  16  15  14

First Random House Edition
STEP INTO READING, RANDOM HOUSE, and the Random House colophon are registered trademarks of Random House, Inc.

# Barbie™
# One Pink Shoe

by Salile Orr
illustrated by S.I. International

Random House 🏠 New York

One, two.

One pink shoe!

Three, four.

Close the door.

Five, six.

Match or mix?

Seven, eight.

Don't be late!

Nine, ten.

Pick up Ken!

Barbie, Barbie,

you look great!

Are you ready

for our date?

Time goes by
way too fast.

But memories

will always last.

Ten, nine.

Wait in line!

Eight, seven.

# Look! It's Kevin!

Six, five.

Splash and dive!

Four, three.

Look and see!

Two, one.

I have to run!

My one pink shoe!
It was with you.